Candles for the Path

To Leo and Lucas,
May your candles never burn out

xxx

Candles for the broken path

A Letter to My Past Self

Dear Me,

I know you're exhausted. I know you're hurting in ways no one sees. You've spent the last ten years in a marriage that, for all its promises, left you feeling empty. You gave everything—your love, your time, your energy—until there was nothing left for yourself. And now, here you are, standing in the wreckage of what was, trying to figure out who you are without it.

You never thought you'd end up here. A single mother. A woman who feels unworthy, undesirable, like damaged goods. You tell yourself that no one will want you now, that love is for other people, for whole people, not for someone like you—someone broken. And that's why you let him in.

I know why you stayed when the red flags started to show. He told you what you already feared: that no one else would love you, that you were lucky he wanted you at all. And because you already believed it, you let him shape your world. You let him define your worth.

You ignored the way his words chipped away at you, the way he made you feel small. You told yourself it wasn't abuse because he didn't hit you—at least not at first. You made excuses, convinced yourself that this was better than being alone. That this was what you deserved.

But let me tell you something, something I wish you had known back then: you were never unlovable. You were never unworthy. You were just vulnerable. And he saw that.

And one day, you will see it too.

I won't lie to you. Walking away won't be easy. You'll battle fear, doubt, and the urge to turn back. But when you do leave—and you will—you will finally begin to heal. You will learn that love is not supposed to make you afraid. That your worth is not determined by who chooses you. That you were never hard to love—you just loved people who made you believe you were.

And one day, you will look at your reflection and see her again. The woman you thought was lost. The mother who found her strength. The survivor who didn't just escape but rebuilt.

You don't see her yet, but she's there. And she's waiting for you.

With love and courage,

Your Future Self

Prologue: The Candles Will Be Lit

I didn't know what I needed. I only knew that I was scared.

When my husband left, suddenly and without warning, the life I had built shattered around me. I was a single mum with two small children, drowning in unanswered questions and doubts. The nights were the hardest—long stretches of silence where fear crept in, whispering that I would never recover. That no one would want me. That I would never feel whole again.

That's how I ended up at Pat's house.

The clairvoyant was a stranger to me then, just someone who I had been told might have answers. But I wasn't even sure what answers I was looking for. When she opened the door, her first question was simple yet jarring.

"Why are you here?"

I hesitated for a moment before admitting the truth.

"I don't know. I think I just need to know I'm going to be okay."

That's when my grandad came through.

The best man I had ever known. Wise, funny, strong, and kind. We used to go shopping together for his weekly groceries and watch the horse racing. He didn't talk much about the past—especially about my nan, who had passed away when my mum was only two. But when he did, it was rare and precious. I held on to those moments.

Pat led me upstairs and left me alone there for what felt like ages. I sat in the stillness, surrounded by the weight of my thoughts. When she finally returned, she apologised and said, "You came with such a negative aura that I had to ask your grandad what to do. His advice? 'She's strong. Tell her the truth.'"

I thought I was strong. I had survived heartbreak before, hadn't I? I had built a life after being abandoned once. Surely I could do it again.

But then she spoke about my trials—about trust issues, miscarriages, others' reliance on me, the wounds left by my ex-husband—and I felt the walls inside me start to crumble.

"You'll be okay," she said gently. "But it's going to take work. You'll kiss a few frogs before you meet your prince."

That's when she said the words that have stayed with me ever since.

"They lit candles to guide your way, but they blew them out. You aren't ready. Your path is too broken."

I blinked at her, confused. "Who blew them out? What candles?"

"The spirits did," she explained. "To guide you toward your happiness. When you're ready, they'll light them again. To light the way across your broken path."

Those words echoed in my mind long after I left her house. Candles to guide my way. A broken path waiting for light. At the time, I didn't fully understand what she meant. I wasn't ready to. But I would carry those words with me like a quiet promise, a reminder that when the time came—when I was truly ready—the candles would be lit once more.

And when that moment came, I finally saw the light.

Chapter 1: The Beginning – Love or Illusion?

A Shattered Fairytale

I was raised to believe in forever.

My parents had been married for 30 years, and to me, they were the definition of love. They had built a life together, weathered storms, and always seemed to find their way back to each other. I looked at them and thought, that's what marriage is supposed to be. A safe place. A constant.

For years, I held onto that belief like a child clutching a treasured book, convinced I already knew how the story ended—happily ever after. But one day, I turned the page and found that the ink had bled, the words smudged and unreadable. A story I thought was solid and whole was suddenly filled with cracks.

There had been another woman.

It didn't happen all at once. It was a slow unravelling, whispers turning into truths, a shift in the air at home that I couldn't quite put my finger on—until I could. And just like that, the foundation I had trusted crumbled beneath me.

My parents were supposed to be the exception. They were supposed to prove that love could last. But now, I wasn't sure if love was built to last at all.

And though I didn't realise it then, that uncertainty would stay with me. It would shape the way I saw relationships, the way I trusted, the way I held onto people even when I shouldn't have.

Finding Security in a Relationship

When I met the father of my children, I was still carrying that fear, even if I didn't say it out loud.

I was young, but already wary. I had seen how love could collapse, how something that once felt unbreakable could turn to dust. I wanted security, something steady, something that wouldn't disappear when I wasn't looking.

And he gave me that. Or at least, he made me feel like he did.

For most of the ten years we were together, I was happy. We built a life, a family. We had children. We got married. We ticked all the boxes. And isn't that what life is supposed to be? That's what we're told—find someone, settle down, build a future together.

But no one tells you what comes after.

No one tells you that beyond the milestones, beyond the smiles in wedding photos and the birthdays and the family holidays, there's work. That love isn't just something you find—it's something you keep choosing. Something you fight for.

And then one day, he stopped fighting for it.

The truth came slowly, in pieces. A change in his voice when he spoke to me. The way he checked his phone more often, guarding it like a secret. The unexplained late nights, the sudden distance between us, as though he had already started pulling away.

At first, I ignored the signs. Convinced myself I was being paranoid. We had been together for a decade—how could he just throw it all away? We had children. A home. A life.

But deep down, I knew.

And when the truth finally came, when all the suspicions turned into confirmation, something unexpected happened.

I felt relief.

I had spent so long living in the shadow of doubt, questioning my own instincts, making excuses for his coldness, his absences, the feeling that I was no longer enough. When he left, it was like the weight of uncertainty was lifted off my chest. There was no more second-guessing. No more waiting for the truth to find me. It was here. And it had set me free.

Yes, he had chosen someone else. Yes, he had broken our family apart. But in doing so, he had also done something I hadn't been able to do for myself—he had given me a clean break.

I wasn't heartbroken the way people expected me to be. They thought I was in shock, numb from the pain. But I wasn't.

I was strong. And I was a fighter.

I refused to let his betrayal define me.

One day, I took the wedding pictures down—not in sorrow, but with a sense of empowerment. It wasn't an ending to mourn; it was a chapter I was finally closing. With every frame that came off the wall, I reclaimed a piece of myself.

I moved forward. I built a life for my children, for myself.

I thought I was unbreakable this time.

But then, in the quiet moments, when the world wasn't watching, I realised something had been left behind in the wreckage.

I had survived the betrayal. I had proven my strength. But one thing still haunted me—the question of who I was now.

I wasn't just a woman starting over. I was a divorced single mum. A woman with two caesarean scars, stretch marks, and a body that had carried, birthed, and nurtured two children.

And then there was her.

The woman ten years younger. The one he had chosen.

I would stand in front of the mirror, pulling at my skin, tracing the lines of motherhood on my body, wondering how I could ever compete. I wasn't twenty-something anymore. I wasn't untouched by time. I had lived. My body had lived.

Would anyone ever want me again?

That question stayed with me, lurking in the back of my mind even as I threw myself into work, into raising my children, into rebuilding a life that was my own.

And that's why meeting him felt so easy.

We had history. We had gone to school together. It felt familiar, safe—like I was skipping the part where I had to be new to someone again. He already knew me, or at least, that's what I thought.

It felt like a second chance, like the start of something that could finally help me heal.

I thought he would help me rebuild.

But over time, he did the opposite.

Chapter 2: The Illusion Begins

After everything I had been through, meeting someone new should have felt daunting. But with him, it didn't.

I knew him from school. That simple fact seemed to smooth over the cracks in my confidence. It made the idea of meeting up feel safe, familiar—like I was reconnecting with an old friend rather than stepping into the uncertain world of dating.

It had been years since we'd last crossed paths, but that history between us gave me something solid to lean on. I wasn't just a stranger anymore. I wasn't a divorced single mother fumbling through small talk and forced smiles. I was someone he had known before the heartbreak, before the weight of everything life had thrown at me.

I organised drinks early on, eager to reconnect. I needed something light and uncomplicated. And he made it easy.

The night unfolded like a reunion of sorts. We swapped stories about school—about the teachers we had both despised, the classmates we'd lost touch with. He laughed as he reminisced about how close he had been to my twin brother, and for a moment, it felt like the years had melted away. We weren't two adults carrying the baggage of broken relationships; we were just two people sharing a slice of nostalgia.

There was something comforting in that. Something I hadn't realised I needed.

But it wasn't just the nostalgia that caught me off guard. It was him.

I had barely noticed him back in school. He wasn't one of the loud, popular boys—the ones who commanded attention and seemed to live in the spotlight. He had been more reserved, someone who blended into the background. But the man sitting across from me that night was different.

He was confident in a way that felt magnetic. He carried himself with ease, leading the conversation as though it were second nature. He was charming—almost effortlessly so—and I found myself drawn in by the way he spoke, the way he seemed genuinely curious about my life.

I wasn't used to this kind of attention. After my marriage had unravelled, I had spent so much time in survival mode—raising my children, holding myself together for their sake. I had almost forgotten what it felt like to be seen as a woman, not just as a mother or a broken version of my former self.

That night, I felt seen.

He asked me about my work, my children, my life since the divorce. There was a warmth in his tone, an attentiveness that made me feel like my words mattered. He told me about his own life—his job as a roofer, the family connections that had shaped him. His story wasn't particularly dramatic or remarkable, but there was something in its simplicity that appealed to me.

He seemed grounded. Reliable.

I remember thinking, This is what I need.

It wasn't a grand romance or an intense whirlwind. It was easy conversation and laughter and the feeling that maybe, just maybe, I could start to build something new with someone who already understood where I came from.

But illusions are seductive by nature. They blind you with the light they cast, making it impossible to see the shadows they hide.

At the time, I didn't question anything. I didn't scrutinise his stories or search for inconsistencies in his words. He seemed sincere, and I wanted to believe he was exactly who he presented himself to be.

How could I have known that the man I was sitting across from wasn't real? That the confident, charming version of himself he offered me that night was a performance designed to disarm me?

But in those early moments, I didn't see the lies.

I saw hope. I saw a possibility I hadn't dared to dream of in years—that maybe this was the beginning of something good.

I let myself believe it.

For the first time in what felt like forever, I wasn't bracing for heartbreak. I wasn't walking on eggshells. I was letting my guard down, allowing myself to feel again.

It's funny how, when you're starved of something for so long, you barely notice when you settle for scraps.

But I didn't see it that way. Not yet.

To me, that night was perfect in its simplicity. I left feeling lighter, warmer, as though I had taken a small but significant step toward reclaiming a piece of myself. I didn't know it then, but that night would become a reference point—a moment I would cling to when things began to unravel.

For now, though, there were no warning signs. No red flags flapping in the corners of my vision. Just the quiet optimism of someone who wanted to believe in new beginnings.

Chapter 3: The Cracks Beneath the Surface

In the beginning, it was easy to believe in him.

I had let my guard down, convinced that this could be the fresh start I needed. He seemed grounded, confident, and sincere. But illusions only hold up for so long. The cracks always find a way to show themselves.

The first fracture came with a revelation I wasn't prepared for.

He didn't have a job.

The confident roofer with his stories of long working hours and building projects had lied. The truth unravelled slowly, each excuse or contradiction widening the gap between the version of him I thought I knew and the reality standing in front of me.

It hit me harder than I expected. It wasn't just about the lie itself—it was the memories it dragged back with it. The echoes of my marriage, of the struggles I had already endured, came flooding back. I had fought so hard to build a stable life for myself and my children after my ex-husband walked away. Now, here I was, staring down the same fear: the possibility that I might have to carry the weight of a relationship all over again.

I should have walked away then.

But I didn't.

I tried to rationalise it. He had been through his own battles—mental health struggles that had left him with scars of his own. He spoke about rebuilding himself, about trying to grow stronger and get his life back on track. Maybe that was why he had lied. Maybe he had been ashamed.

I convinced myself that perhaps I could be part of his growth, that we could help each other heal. I clung to the hope that things could still work out. I wanted to believe it so badly. The truth was, I was terrified.

The idea of starting over in the dating world felt overwhelming. I didn't know how to date or meet new people. I was scared of being alone, scared that I might never find someone who would want me—someone with two children and scars that told the story of their birth. So, I clung to what I had, desperately searching for positives to hold onto.

But the cracks kept appearing.

It wasn't just the lie about his job. There were other things—small things, at first. The way he drank, not just socially but excessively. And then there were the comments.

"Why don't you come to the gym with me?"

"Are you going to wear that top?"

They seemed harmless in the moment. He always said them with a smile or a teasing tone that made it easy to brush off. But each time, they burrowed deeper into my mind, planting seeds of doubt. Was I out of shape? Was I dressing wrong? These weren't things I had worried about before, but now they felt like flaws I needed to fix.

Bit by bit, he was picking me apart, making me question things I had never questioned before.

Still, I convinced myself it wasn't that bad.

And then, he met my children.

I was nervous about introducing them to him. My kids were everything to me, and the thought of letting someone into that part of my life felt like a huge risk. But he was good with them.

He took Leo outside to play basketball, encouraging him with patience and laughter. He cuddled up with Lucas, sharing quiet moments on the sofa as they watched something on the iPad together. It was such a simple, gentle scene, but it meant the world to me.

For a while, I let myself believe that he truly cared for them.

I told myself that a man who was willing to take on not just me but my children had to be someone special.

The doubts and warning signs didn't disappear, but they faded into the background. I was so desperate to believe in this relationship that I ignored the alarms blaring in my mind. I told myself that maybe my expectations were too high. After all, who was I to demand perfection?

I thought I was lucky that he had chosen me—that he was willing to accept my circumstances.

But the truth I couldn't admit to myself at the time was that my expectations weren't high at all. They were painfully low. I had become so accustomed to feeling unworthy that I settled for anyone who would take me, flaws and all.

I wish someone had slapped me with the truth—reminded me of what I was worth. That I didn't have to settle for scraps of love and acceptance. That I was enough, just as I was.

But at that point, I didn't see it.

All I saw was someone who, for better or worse, was willing to be with me. And so, I stayed.

Chapter 4: The Mask Begins to Slip

For a time, everything seemed perfect—almost too perfect.

When he introduced me to his family and friends, I was drawn into a world that felt safe and inviting. His family welcomed me with open arms, and his friends were easy-going and friendly, always ready to include me in plans and conversations. It was as if I had stepped into a carefully crafted bubble of support.

There were barbecues on weekends, group outings, and long conversations that left me feeling reassured and accepted. I wasn't just meeting him; I was becoming part of something bigger.

I didn't realise at the time how much I craved that feeling. After my divorce, I had been locked in survival mode, focused entirely on raising my children and holding myself together. I hadn't let myself imagine what it might feel like to belong again.

It wasn't just about him anymore. It was about all of them.

With every warm smile, every friendly invitation, I felt the fear and insecurity I had carried for so long start to retreat. I told myself that this was different. He wasn't just offering me love—he was offering me a community, a second chance at the life I had lost.

But there was a quiet discomfort beneath it all. An itch at the back of my mind, subtle but persistent. Something didn't feel quite right, though I couldn't put my finger on it. I brushed it aside, convincing myself that I was overthinking.

Then came the trip to Spain.

I should have been excited. I was introducing him to my mum and stepdad—two of the most important people in my life. But as the trip drew closer, that discomfort grew. It was a strange, gnawing feeling, almost like claustrophobia. It felt as though I were walking into something I couldn't quite control.

When we arrived, I plastered on a smile, determined to make everything go smoothly. But my mum's reaction was immediate. She saw through him the moment they met.

There was no warmth in her eyes when she spoke to him. No polite pretense. She wasn't one to mince words or soften her opinions for anyone's benefit. She disliked him, and she made no effort to hide it.

"He's not what he seems," she told me later, her voice firm and sure.

Her words hit me like a slap.

For 33 years, I had trusted her instincts. She had always been my role model, my source of truth. If she saw something off about him, I knew deep down that she was right. But I didn't want her to be. I had invested too much in the idea of him. I didn't want to believe that the bubble I had stepped into was built on a lie.

Instead of facing the truth, I panicked.

I spent the rest of the trip walking on eggshells, trying to smooth over the tension between him and my family. I told myself that maybe she was being too harsh, that she didn't understand him the way I did.

But the unease followed me home.

Back in the UK, I found myself avoiding the truth in the only way I knew how—by picking fights with her. Every little comment she made sparked an argument. I told myself it was her fault, that she was overstepping. But deep down, I knew I was trying to push her away. It was easier to fight her than to confront the cracks forming in my relationship with him.

And that's exactly what he needed.

It wasn't long before he began planting doubts in my mind.

"Why does your mum always have something to say about us?"

"Your friends don't really understand your life like I do, do they?"

At first, the comments seemed innocent enough—expressions of concern, subtle nudges meant to make me think twice about the people around me. But gradually, they grew more pointed. He framed himself as my closest ally, the one person who truly understood me. The doubts he sowed took root slowly, until I began second-guessing the people I had trusted most.

I started making excuses not to see my family and friends. The arguments with my mum became more frequent, more intense. He would be there to comfort me after each one, quietly reinforcing the idea that maybe she wasn't as supportive as I thought.

"You can't let her control your life," he'd say softly. "You're strong enough to stand on your own."

It was insidious, the way he isolated me. I didn't see it for what it was at the time. I thought I was making my own choices—distancing myself from conflict, prioritising the relationship I was trying to build.

By the time I realised how much space had grown between me and the people I cared about, it was too late. The wedge had been driven deep, and he was firmly in control of the narrative.

Looking back, I see those moments for what they were. My mum had been the first person to see through the mask he wore, and that terrified me. I had chosen denial over truth, fear over confrontation. And it cost me more than I could have imagined.

Chapter 5: The Turning Point

For a while, everything seemed to be falling into place.

Leo was seven and starting to explore gaming—something I knew absolutely nothing about. Give me football sidelines and muddy boots any day, but ask me to sort out a PlayStation or Nintendo console and I'd run for the hills. Thankfully, he knew exactly what to do. He was clued up, brought over an old PS4 for Leo to keep, and helped set up usernames and passwords. We linked it to my Apple ID and payment details for those never-ending purchases of 'vbucks.' (Oh, the eye rolls.)

It was a small thing, but it mattered. He filled in a gap I didn't know how to handle. My kids were happy, and that was all that mattered to me at the time. It gave me a sense of relief, another reason to believe that he was the person I needed. Someone to solve problems I couldn't. Someone who would stay.

But I did warn you, didn't I? My expectations were low.

The cracks came slowly at first, subtle enough that I could justify them away. But then, like with so many things, they widened.

It started with one decision—a decision made in fear. I had planned to meet an old friend for a drink. Over the years of working in education, I had built close friendships—like second families in each school I worked in. This friend was one of those people, someone I hadn't seen in a long time. But I knew, instinctively, that if I told him where I was going that night, there would be an argument.

Why? Because my friend was male.

The thought of that fight kept me silent. I hated the feeling of sneaking around, of making excuses and hiding plans. I had grown up surrounded by male friends because of my twin brother, Chris. They had always been a comforting presence in my life. Yet now, I was being made to feel as though these friendships were something I had to hide.

It wasn't me. It wasn't the person I had always been.

But I ignored that feeling and went to the pub anyway.

We met at a small, familiar spot and fell into easy conversation. We laughed about old times, swapped parenting horror stories, and joked about the absurdity of growing older. Hours passed without us noticing. It felt good to talk to someone who knew me—really knew me—without any hidden agendas. For those few hours, I felt like myself again.

We were just debating whether to order one last drink when I saw him.

He stormed into the pub like a thundercloud, his face dark and twisted with anger. My heart dropped into my stomach. I hadn't told him where I was. How did he know?

And he wasn't alone. His friends hung back near the entrance, watching but not interfering. Their presence felt ominous, like silent enforcers.

I froze. Every muscle in my body tensed as he moved closer, his eyes locked on mine. The pub, once warm and buzzing with life, now felt suffocating. The noise faded into the background as panic took hold.

The comments began immediately—derogatory, humiliating, and loud enough for others to hear. My skin burned with shame. I had never been spoken to like that before, reduced to labels that felt like daggers.

I turned to my friend, trying to keep my voice steady despite the trembling in my hands.

"You should go," I said quietly. "I'll sort this."

He hesitated, concern flashing in his eyes. "Are you sure?"

I nodded, forcing a smile I didn't feel. "I'll be fine."

Reluctantly, he left. I watched him walk away, feeling the weight of the situation settle heavily on my shoulders. I followed shortly after, desperate to escape. But he wasn't done with me yet.

He followed me out to the car park.

The cold night air hit me like a slap, but it did nothing to calm the rising fear in my chest. I walked quickly, trying to create distance, but his footsteps echoed close behind.

"How did you know where I was?" I finally asked, my voice barely more than a whisper.

He stopped beside me, his face a mask of cold detachment. "Your location," he said flatly. "I hacked your Apple ID and found your location."

The words were delivered with an eerie calmness, as if he had just told me the time. There was no emotion—no anger, no remorse—just a chilling indifference.

My mind reeled. He had hacked my phone. He had guessed my password. The same details I had shared with him for Leo's gaming setup had been turned into a weapon. He had used that trust to track me, to control me. To hunt me down.

I felt sick. My hands shook as I tried to process what he had just said, but there was no time.

We kept walking, the tension between us palpable. My phone buzzed in my hand—messages from my friend, checking if I was okay. It was a lifeline I couldn't hold onto.

He grabbed the phone and smashed it to the ground. The screen shattered on impact, splintering into dozens of jagged pieces. Without hesitation, he stomped on it repeatedly, crushing the last remnants of my connection to the outside world.

Adrenaline surged through me. I sprinted the last few steps to my car and locked the doors with shaking hands. The engine roared to life, but any sense of safety was short-lived.

The pounding started.

He was outside, slamming his fists against the windows with a fury that shook the entire car. Each blow reverberated through my body, a terrifying rhythm that wouldn't stop. I braced myself, gripping the steering wheel as glass shattered around me. The passenger window exploded, sending shards flying into my lap.

I didn't think. I just acted.

I pressed the accelerator and sped out of the car park, my heart racing, my body trembling. Tiny pieces of glass dug into my skin, but I barely noticed. I didn't know where I was going—I only knew I couldn't go home. I couldn't go to a friend's house. He already knew too much.

The safety I had once felt in his presence was gone.

Replaced by fear.

Chapter 6: The Aftermath

"Amy, you need to call the police."

His voice broke through the haze like a sharp gust of wind. I blinked, momentarily disoriented. Where was I?

As he kept talking, the events of the past few hours came rushing back like a tidal wave. The pub. The car park. The shattering glass. The pounding on the windows. I had driven blindly, desperate for safety, and ended up here—at my ex-husband's house.

It was the one place I could go where I knew he couldn't find me. He didn't know this address. He didn't know where my children spent half their time.

I watched as my ex-husband moved outside, taping up my broken windows with bin liners and duct tape. The wind howled around him, pulling at the flimsy plastic, but he worked methodically, his movements steady. It was a temporary fix, but in that moment, it felt like a lifeline.

I sat on the sofa, numb, staring at him through the window. My mind raced with fragmented thoughts. I had felt relieved when he had left me. We had drifted apart, and I never would have been the one to walk away. But now, here I was—seeking safety from someone far worse.

This was something deeper than heartbreak.

Something that felt like a cancer. It had spread quietly, without me fully realising it, until it consumed everything. Pain and destruction. That's what he had brought into my life. And now, I felt stuck, trapped in a nightmare with no clear way out.

I wanted to scream those words into the night. But I didn't. Not yet. They remained an awful truth that I kept to myself, too afraid to give them life by saying them aloud.

When he finished, my ex-husband came back inside, his expression serious but gentle. He sat down beside me and said it again, firmly this time.

"Amy, you need to call the police."

I didn't argue. I knew he was right. I watched as he picked up his phone and dialled, staying by my side, holding my hand through the entire process.

The words felt surreal as I recounted the story to the officer on the other end of the line. It was like telling someone else's story—like I had stepped outside myself and was observing from a distance.

I cried until there were no tears left.

Eventually, I went home. I don't remember much about the drive. The exhaustion was bone-deep, numbing every part of me. I walked into the house like a ghost, moving on autopilot. I collapsed into bed without even changing out of my clothes.

The days that followed were a blur. Everyone around me was supportive, but there was an unspoken question behind their concerned eyes: How did you let this happen?

No one said it aloud, but I could feel it—like a whisper in the back of my mind. It was the question I had already been asking myself.

I wasn't stupid. I was educated. I was successful. I was a good mum. So why had I ended up here? What had I become?

The shame weighed heavily on me, suffocating.

I thought I could fix things. I thought if I pressed charges, it would send a message. That he would know I wasn't weak, that I wasn't someone he could throw around and break. I was determined to prove that to myself and everyone else.

But then I dropped the charges.

I've questioned that decision more times than I can count. Why did I do it? Why didn't I stay strong? Maybe if I had, it all would have ended there. Maybe things would never have escalated.

But I didn't stay strong. I gave in.

And that's the part so many people don't understand. The invisible hold they have over you—it's real. It's not something you can just shake off with a stern look in the mirror or a pep talk from a friend. It's deep and all-encompassing, weaving itself into every corner of your mind until it feels like you can't breathe without their permission.

I had thought I was strong.

But strength takes many forms. I hadn't yet found the strength to break free from him entirely. Not then.

I told myself that things might still get better. That maybe I could regain control. But deep down, I knew the truth.

The path ahead was broken.

And I still wasn't ready to light the candles that would guide my way.

Chapter 7: The Depths of Control

If you had asked me if things could get worse after that night, I would have said no.

Surely, shattered windows and a public display of rage was the worst it could get. But abuse isn't that simple. It adapts, morphing into something less visible but equally destructive. He calmed after the incident, at least on the surface.

But that word—calm—was deceptive. The violence may have paused, but his control only tightened.

It's terrifying how your mind starts to recalibrate danger. I caught myself doing it all the time. The broken windows were a "10." So when he did something new—maybe intimidation, maybe a verbal attack—I'd rate it in my mind. A "7." Maybe a "6." And if it wasn't as bad as a "10," I convinced myself it was okay.

Sickening, isn't it? How you start measuring your pain and fear on a scale, as if that makes it any more tolerable.

Bit by bit, his claws sank deeper. I became numb to it, retreating inward as a means of survival. He manipulated every part of my life.

He tried adding my male friends on Instagram, men who had been in my life for years. When they saw his erratic behaviour—the possessiveness, the rage—they blocked me without a second thought. It wasn't worth the risk for them.

He critiqued how I did simple, daily things—how I cleaned, how I organised the house. So I stopped doing them. He criticised my parenting, pointing out flaws that weren't there. I changed my style, adapting to his warped expectations just to avoid the comments.

The more I lost control, the more his voice took over. His control wasn't just in the words he spoke; it seeped into every action I took, every decision I made.

Pat's words echoed in my mind during those moments: You haven't found your prince yet.

No, I hadn't. But calling him a frog felt too simplistic.

Then things took an unexpected turn. He had a strange habit of mentioning his exes—a lot. I never fully understood why. Was it to intimidate me? To remind me that he had "options"? Maybe he wanted me to feel small, to be grateful that he had chosen me at all. Or maybe it was designed to toy with my insecurities, the ones that still lingered after my marriage fell apart.

Whatever the reason, it worked. The idea of these other women haunted me.

One day, I decided I needed answers. I bit the bullet and reached out to one of them. I already knew quite a bit about her—more than I should have. She was a single mum like me. She seemed to have a similar personality, the kind of woman I might have befriended in other circumstances.

I don't even remember what that first message said. But I remember her reply.

It wasn't text. It was a voice note.

I paused, puzzled. Voice notes weren't exactly my go-to for messaging. But as the conversation unfolded, the reason became clear.

She didn't want anything traceable. A voice note couldn't be screenshotted or easily shared.

She was scared.

I could hear it in her voice—the hesitation, the fear of saying too much. She was worried that whatever she shared might find its way back to him. That we were caught in some twisted, sick game he had orchestrated.

And that's exactly what she admitted to me.

As our conversation flowed, piece by piece, her story came out. It was a horror show. The abuse she endured far surpassed what I had experienced, yet it still resonated with me on a deeply personal level. It was like hearing an echo of my own life, amplified by time and trauma.

I thought my chapter was dark.

Her story revealed just how deep the shadows could go.

I met her, secretly.

We arranged the meeting like we were planning something dangerous, as though we were still under his watchful eye. It was strange, sitting across from someone who had lived a parallel version of my life. Someone who knew exactly what it was like without needing me to explain.

We shared stories—painful ones—but somehow, we found moments of laughter in the pain. There's a certain absurdity to trauma that only those who've endured it can truly understand. We laughed at the tactics he used, the ridiculous things he said to keep us under his thumb.

Then she mentioned something that stuck with me: a podcast. She said it had helped her through the worst of it, and I should listen to it. It focused on gaslighting—on people who manipulate and twist reality to maintain control.

"An egotistical gas-lighter," she called him.

She wasn't wrong. The podcast opened my eyes to what I had been living through. There was one motif that resonated above all else: breadcrumbs.

They leave you breadcrumbs. Little positive moments scattered through the darkness, just enough for you to cling to. When the abuse is at its worst, you remind yourself of those moments—of the way they smiled at you once, the way they held your hand after a bad day—and convince yourself that things aren't that bad. That they do have a beautiful side.

Breadcrumbs.

I saw them everywhere now. Every time he did something kind, every time he apologised and promised to change, I recognised it for what it was. A breadcrumb.

I really liked her. But I was angry. Furious, even.

She had been through this. She had seen the worst of him, and yet she had done nothing. Fear had kept her silent—fear of him, fear of his family, fear of the threats he had made. And I hated that. I hated that she had let it happen.

But then I remembered the smashed windows. The dropped charges.

Who was I to judge her?

I was a hypocrite, sitting there raging at her fear when I had been just as paralysed by my own.

Still, the rage lingered, aimed more at the situation than at her. I couldn't let this cycle continue. I couldn't let there be a third victim.

But I didn't know how to stop it.

The breadcrumbs were powerful. They shouldn't have been. They were tiny, fragile things—crumbs that should have crumbled to dust at the slightest touch. You couldn't build anything with them. You couldn't hold them in your hands without them breaking apart.

Yet somehow, these small, broken fragments held immense power. They had become an invisible force, imprisoning me within walls I couldn't even see.

Chapter 8: The Final Straw

I had moments of clarity; glimpses of what life might be like without him. But then fear and hope pulled me back. The breadcrumbs always worked their magic—those fleeting, deceptive moments of kindness and affection. They created a distorted reality where I kept convincing myself that things weren't that bad.

I told myself that people didn't understand. They saw snapshots—moments of chaos and control—but they didn't live inside it. I did. I understood its complexities. That's what I told myself, anyway.

But deep down, I knew. I knew I needed to escape. The problem was figuring out how.

I leaned on others more, though cautiously. My close friends started picking up on the signs, and my mum—her eyes carried the truth I still wasn't ready to face. The ex I'd reached out to had become an ally of sorts. We didn't talk often, but when we did, there was a sense of mutual understanding that needed no words.

The turning point came when he planned a night away. I didn't know how things would unravel that night, how the image he had so carefully maintained would collapse entirely.

It started off fine, almost pleasant. We checked into a hotel, had dinner, and even shared a few laughs. For a moment, I let myself believe this could be one of those good nights, a breadcrumb to cling to.

Then we went to a club.

At first, he was in his element. He made friends easily, chatting with the bouncer at the entrance, buying drinks, pulling me onto the dance floor. But as the night wore on, something shifted. His mood darkened, paranoia creeping in like a shadow.

"He took your number, didn't he?"

"What?" I blinked, caught off guard. "No, of course not."

"Don't lie to me," he snarled, his face twisted with fury. "You were flirting with him!"

It was absurd. He had been the one who started talking to the bouncer, yet here I was, under fire for something that hadn't happened.

His rage escalated. He was barred from the club shortly after, his outburst catching the attention of security.

We returned to the hotel in tense silence. As we made our way down the corridor to our room, he snapped.

"Slag," he muttered under his breath, the word cutting through the quiet.

I didn't react. I kept walking, desperate to avoid a confrontation.

But he wasn't done. He shoved me—hard—sending me stumbling forward. I caught myself just before I hit the floor, my wrist taking the brunt of the impact.

A shooting pain shot up my arm. I gasped softly, trying to shrug it off. My hand throbbed, but I focused on steadying my breath. I didn't want him to see me cry.

But he saw.

"Whore," he spat.

Tears stung my eyes. I blinked them away, telling myself to stay calm.

Then came the final blow.

"No wonder he left you. No wonder he cheated on you."

The words hit harder than the push had. I had heard them before—too many times. They echoed every fear and insecurity I had tried to bury since my marriage ended.

But this time, something changed.

The pain in my wrist, the tears threatening to fall, the echo of his words... all of it crystallised into one undeniable truth: I was done.

I barely slept that night. I lay awake in the darkness, listening to the distant hum of the hotel. My mind raced, piecing together every breadcrumb, every manipulation, every moment of fear. The push in the corridor had broken something in me, but strangely, it had also rebuilt something.

By morning, I knew.

I was done.

I checked my phone, still groggy from lack of sleep. That's when I noticed something strange. My Hive heating system had been active during the night. It had gone into overdrive, heating the house to a level I never set. I never left the heating on overnight.

Odd, I thought, but I didn't dwell on it.

We drove back in silence. I kept my thoughts to myself, rehearsing the conversation I knew I needed to have. About an hour into the drive, I pulled into a service station. It was time.

"We need to talk," I said, breaking the quiet that had hung between us like a heavy fog. "This is it. We need a clean break. No hard feelings. I'll drop you home, and that'll be that."

He didn't say much, and for a brief moment, I thought it might actually go smoothly.

Then my phone rang.

I ignored it at first. Then it rang again.

By the third call, I knew something was wrong. I answered, my voice cautious.

"Hello?"

It was my neighbour—a man I had known for years.

"Amy, I've just driven past your house," he said, his voice laced with urgency. "All the doors are open. I think you've been burgled. Shall I go in?"

The words hit me like a punch to the gut. My mind raced, connecting dots that had been scattered moments before. The Hive system. The heating turning on in the middle of the night.

I couldn't be sure he was involved, but the feeling clawed at me, that gnawing suspicion. I could almost hear him planting his next move, his voice saying, I'll protect you. I'm here for you.

That wasn't the worst part, though.

The worst part was how quickly he jumped into saviour mode, his invisible cape firmly on. I had found my way out. And now, he had found the perfect way back in.

Chapter 9: A Home in Ruins

I wasn't prepared for what I saw when we got back.

The house I had worked so hard to build as a safe haven was unrecognisable. Doors hung wide open, and the chaos spilled out onto the driveway. Inside, it was worse. Black paint had been splattered everywhere, staining walls and furniture. Drawers had been emptied, belongings either stolen or destroyed. The carpets were soaked in places, as if whoever had done this wanted to ruin every last thing.

I stood there, frozen, unable to comprehend the destruction around me.

The police questioned me, their voices blending into the background noise of my thoughts. Was it a hate crime? They asked. Did I have any enemies? I shook my head, barely able to respond. None of this made sense.

His family arrived soon after. They flew in quickly, all concern and offers of help. It was strange how fast they mobilised, how eager they were to take control of the situation. Something didn't feel right, but I was too numb to question it at the time.

As we sat around the kitchen table, I stared blankly at the mess surrounding us. The abuser's voice grated in my ears, an endless stream of complaints about his broken oven.

"I'm going to have to buy microwave food now," he groaned dramatically.

I blinked, trying to register his words. He was standing in my destroyed house—where every inch of my life had been upturned—and he was complaining about his oven.

I couldn't believe what I was hearing.

But it got worse.

In front of my best friend, who had come to support me, he leaned against the counter and casually asked, "Have you ever watched Luther? They could still be here, you know—hiding in the loft."

His words hit like a slap.

There I was, sitting in shock, surrounded by the remnants of my life, and he was making a joke about intruders. As if this were entertainment.

Thankfully, my best friend didn't hold back.

"What the hell is wrong with you?" she snapped, her voice cutting through the heavy silence. "This isn't a joke! Look around you!"

I stayed silent, still too stunned to react. I felt like a spectator in my own life, watching the scene unfold from a distance.

Her anger echoed what I couldn't bring myself to say.

After that day, fear became a constant presence in my life. The thought of being alone in that house, of walking through rooms that no longer felt like mine, filled me with dread. Every noise made my heart race. I jumped at shadows, convinced someone could be hiding in the dark corners of my home.

And he knew.

He slipped back into the role of protector as if it were second nature. His family rallied around, creating a sense of support I desperately needed but didn't trust. They made sure I wasn't alone, always present, always watching. He offered to stay with me, insisting it was for my safety.

At a time when I was at my most vulnerable, he found a way back into my life. His invisible cape was back on, and I was too scared and too exhausted to push him away.

But he didn't just offer emotional support. He was meticulous in dealing with the aftermath, especially with the insurance claim. I barely knew where to start—everything was overwhelming. The forms, the assessments, the phone calls to insurance agents. My mind was fogged by fear and exhaustion, and just thinking about the process made me want to curl up in a ball.

He, on the other hand, thrived on the details. He took control with a calm efficiency that both reassured and unnerved me. He walked through the house with a notebook, jotting down every single piece of damage. Black paint on the walls? Check. Missing electronics? Documented.

"You'll need to list everything," he said, almost clinically, as he guided me through the next steps. "It's the only way they'll pay out what you're owed."

He called the insurance company on my behalf, asking all the right questions. He followed up with agents, scheduled appointments for assessors to visit, and made sure every aspect of the claim was handled down to the smallest detail. I knew that without him, it would have taken me weeks to even begin untangling the paperwork.

And for that, I was grateful.

It was a task that had to be done, and he was doing it flawlessly. I watched as he organised receipts, created lists, and negotiated with the insurance representatives. I told myself this was just practical—he was good at this, and I needed the help.

But there was a cost.

With each day that passed, his presence became more entrenched. His meticulous nature, the very thing making the insurance process bearable, was also a reminder of how deeply he could embed himself into my life. He framed it all as a selfless act—"I'm just here to help you," he would say.

Yet I couldn't shake the feeling that this was more than just support. This was control disguised as care. Each piece of paperwork he filed, each phone call he made, was another string tying him back into my world.

He didn't need to yell or shove to reassert his power. This was a subtler manipulation, one that preyed on my vulnerabilities. I needed the insurance claim to be resolved. I needed to rebuild my home, my life. And he knew that.

The fear of being alone, of handling everything on my own, kept me quiet. Kept me in his orbit.

I told myself it was temporary. Just until the paperwork was done. Just until the house was repaired. But deep down, I knew how easily this could become permanent. I had walked this road before.

And once again, I found myself questioning how I had gotten here. The breadcrumbs kept me from seeing the full picture, making me cling to those moments of "helpfulness," as though they outweighed the damage he had already caused.

But even as I sat in the wreckage of my home, something inside me whispered that this time, I couldn't let him stay.

I just needed to find the strength to listen.

Chapter 10: The Monster Unleashed

It didn't happen all at once.

The violence built slowly over time, hidden beneath layers of small incidents that seemed easy to dismiss. He'd throw something across the room—just frustration, I told myself. He'd punch a wall—better the wall than me, right? I tried to rationalise it. But each of those moments left scars on the house, and on me.

His hallway told the real story: holes in the plaster like gaping wounds. I learned to walk past them without looking, pretending they didn't matter. But I felt them, like silent warnings. The tension in the air grew thicker each day, and I waited for the moment it would explode.

Then came the drinking. His temper became a volatile force, barely contained. One wrong word, one perceived slight, and he would unravel. I tried to stay calm, to manage the storm. I thought I could handle it—until that night at the pub.

The evening began like so many others. We'd gone out to "unwind." He'd had a rough day, or so he said. His version of unwinding meant drink after drink, each one erasing the line between civility and chaos.

I saw it in his eyes—the way he scanned the room, tense and restless. He was on edge, seeking conflict. I stayed quiet, hoping to keep the peace. But trouble always found him.

It started with an argument near the bar. Words flew like daggers, and before I could react, the fight spilled outside.

I didn't want to see it.

The thought of fighting made my stomach turn. The sound of fists colliding, the animalistic grunts, the shouted threats—it was all too much. I couldn't bear to watch. I turned away, walking in the opposite direction, ashamed to be connected to him. I didn't care where I was going. I just needed to get away.

Memories swirled as I walked.

Pat's voice... her warnings.

"They lit candles to guide you, but your path is too broken."

How many times had I ignored the signs? How many moments had I brushed aside, convincing myself that it wasn't that bad?

But this time, something was different. The atmosphere was thick with tension, like the air before a storm. I could feel it creeping up behind me.

Then the footsteps.

They were fast, urgent, closing the distance between us in seconds. I barely had time to turn before his hand was around my throat.

The world tilted as he lifted me off the ground.

At first, I didn't even register what was happening. My mind couldn't process it. Then the pain came—sharp and suffocating. His grip tightened, cutting off my air. I kicked and clawed at his arm, panic flooding every inch of my body.

I gasped, but no air came. My lungs screamed. Black spots danced in my vision.

This is how it ends…

I thought of my boys. Of the life I was supposed to be living, the woman I used to be. I couldn't die like this, in the middle of a street, over something so senseless.

Then I heard a voice.

"It's okay, I saw the whole thing!"

The grip on my throat released, and I crumpled to the ground, coughing violently. I gulped in air, my throat burning. My knees scraped against the pavement, and I winced as pain shot through my legs.

I blinked up at the figure standing over me.

It was a woman. As my vision cleared, I recognised her face—someone we had gone to school with.

Relief and shame collided inside me. I didn't know whether to thank her or hide from her.

"Are you okay?" she asked softly, her eyes full of concern.

I nodded, though I wasn't sure if I believed it. I was still shaking, my hands trembling uncontrollably.

She crouched beside me. "Do you want me to call someone?"

"No," I croaked, my voice barely audible. "I'll be fine."

She didn't push, though I could see the doubt in her eyes. Behind us, he stood frozen, his face a mask of confusion and anger. He didn't say a word. Maybe he finally realised he had gone too far.

I wanted to disappear. The weight of her gaze, the unspoken questions—Why haven't you left him? Why are you still here? —pressed down on me like a heavy blanket.

I didn't have answers. Not ones I could say out loud.

That night should have been the end. It should have been the moment I walked away, never to return. But it wasn't.

He apologised, as he always did. Said he didn't remember what had happened. He blamed the alcohol, promised it wouldn't happen again. And like a fool, I forgave him.

Forgiving him that night seemed to unlock something darker. It was as if I had given him permission to fully unleash the monster inside. The violence became more frequent, more brazen. Objects flew across rooms, smashing against walls. His voice, once filled with manipulative charm, now carried an unmistakable menace.

The monster had taken over.

And I became desensitised to it.

Each outburst became another mark on my internal scale of danger. If it wasn't as bad as the choking incident or the shattered windows, I convinced myself I could handle it. I survived by shutting down, by detaching from the horror around me.

But I was crumbling.

The fear that once paralysed me had been replaced by numbness. I moved through life like a ghost, disconnected from myself and everyone I loved. The strong, independent woman who had rebuilt her life after divorce was gone.

In her place was someone who had learned to endure.

I wasn't living. I was surviving. And the monster wasn't going to let me go without a fight.

Chapter 11: Living the Lie

I wish I could say the attack outside the pub changed everything. That it snapped me awake, that I walked away and never looked back. But that's not how it happened.

Instead, I sank deeper into the lie I was living.

It was a slow descent. I told myself it wasn't as bad as it seemed. I became numb to the fear, numb to the violence. It became part of the routine, another thread woven into the fabric of my days. I stopped questioning it. Stopped hoping. I let the resignation settle into my bones.

Maybe this was my life now.

Friends and family tried to reach out, but I could feel the distance between us widening. They didn't understand why I stayed. Their concern began to shift into quiet frustration, their expressions harder, their questions sharper.

"You need to leave," my best friend said one day. Her voice was firm but tinged with desperation, like she didn't know how many more times she could have this conversation with me.

I nodded, muttered something about needing to sort things out first. We both knew it was a lie.

Their questions haunted me.

Why don't you just leave?
How can you let him treat you like this?
What happened to you?

I didn't have answers that would make sense to anyone outside the nightmare I was living. How could I explain the invisible chains that held me in place? The constant cycle of fear and manipulation that left me paralysed?

The shame was overwhelming. I could see it in their eyes—the silent judgment. They thought I was weak. Maybe I was.

But it wasn't just their voices I heard. There were voices in my own mind, relentless and cruel.

You're not strong enough.
You'll never get out.
This is your life now.

Those thoughts followed me everywhere. I carried them like a weight on my chest, crushing and suffocating. The fear of leaving wasn't just about him—it was about me. About the fear of being alone.

I'd been alone once before, after my marriage ended. The loneliness had consumed me, leaving me vulnerable and broken. When he came into my life, it felt like salvation at the time. But now I was trapped, tethered to someone who was slowly destroying me.

He knew how much I feared the isolation. He used it against me in subtle, insidious ways.

"You wouldn't survive on your own," he'd say, his voice calm, almost casual. "You can't even handle things without me."

Those words echoed in my mind long after he said them, feeding every insecurity I had. I believed him. I believed that I wasn't capable of standing on my own.

And so, I stayed.

The days became a blur. I woke up each morning and braced myself for whatever version of him I might encounter. Would it be the man who promised to change? The man who brought me coffee and told me I was beautiful? Or would it be the monster? The man whose temper could turn on a dime, whose rage filled every corner of the room?

It was exhausting, living on the edge of uncertainty. I stopped looking for ways out. Stopped fighting.

Every now and then, I'd think about the past. I'd think about Pat, the clairvoyant, and the things she had told me that day.

"They lit candles to guide you, but your path is broken."

At the time, I hadn't fully understood what she meant. Now, I did. My path was shattered, and I couldn't see a way forward. I didn't know if I ever would.

Then something changed.

I didn't feel strong, but I began to recognise that I couldn't live like this forever. Deep down, a small voice whispered that there was still a way out. Slowly, tentatively, I started to plan.

I set the summer as my target.

I didn't tell him, of course. I couldn't risk him knowing. But I booked a trip to Spain—just me and the boys. It would be our escape, our celebration of freedom. I pictured the sun warming my skin, the boys laughing on the beach. It became my beacon, something to hold onto during the darkest moments.

But planning an escape meant being careful. I couldn't leave all at once. He would notice, and his temper would flare. So I started small.

I began removing things from his house—just little items he wouldn't miss.

A pair of joggers one day.
A hairbrush the next.
Then my slippers.

Each item I took felt like reclaiming a piece of myself. I packed them away quietly, hiding them out of sight, hoping he wouldn't notice the gradual disappearance of my belongings.

With each small act, I felt a flicker of control returning to me.

But even with those plans in motion, the weight of my reality bore down on me. One day, after an uplifting day at work—one of the rare moments when I felt capable and confident—I walked into his house expecting a brief moment of peace. Maybe he'd greet me with a coffee, as he sometimes did when things were calm.

Instead, I walked into a void.

The atmosphere was suffocating, heavy with tension. It hit me like a physical force, knocking the air from my lungs.

He wasn't shouting. He didn't need to. The silence was worse.

I stood there, frozen, as the familiar darkness crept back in. Every ounce of positivity I'd carried home from work evaporated in an instant. I was back in the cage, trapped under the weight of his control.

And in that moment, I felt like I couldn't take it anymore.

I wanted to scream, to run, to shatter the suffocating silence that had taken hold of my life. But I didn't.

Instead, I reminded myself of Spain. Of the plan. Of the boys and the life I was trying to rebuild for us.

I told myself that I just had to hold on a little longer.

Just a little longer.

Chapter 12: Breaking Point

I should have known better than to speak too openly that night.

Honesty was always a mistake with him. I knew that, yet I still let my guard slip. Maybe it was because I'd had such a good day at work—resolving problems, feeling capable and strong—that I wanted to hold onto that feeling a little longer. I wanted to believe that strength could carry over into my time with him.

But I didn't think about where I was. I didn't think about him.

"I'm going," I said abruptly, my voice firmer than it had been in a long time. "I arrived in such a good mood, and you... this space... it's so negative, so stifling. I can't stay here."

The words spilled out, raw and unfiltered. They weren't calculated or cautious like they usually were. I wasn't walking on eggshells this time. I had been pushed too far for that.

I started packing up my things, pulling my laptop case out of my bag as if to anchor myself to the decision. I needed to leave. But I should have known it wouldn't be that simple.

The slam echoed through the house.

I didn't flinch. I didn't even turn around. I'd heard it too many times before—doors, cupboards, whatever was nearby. He always found something to take his anger out on.

But the sharp pain that followed caught me completely off guard.

A searing bolt shot through my leg, and I yelped in pain, clutching at it as tears sprang to my eyes. My vision blurred for a moment as I struggled to process what had just happened.

What the hell was that? What did he do?

I looked at him, my leg throbbing as I gently touched the spot where the pain was radiating. Blood was trickling down my shin, and a deep, angry bruise had already started to form. I could barely press against the wound without gasping in pain.

He stood frozen, staring at me. I couldn't read his expression—shock? Anger? Guilt? His eyes locked onto mine, wide and almost vacant. I wouldn't forget that look.

For a moment, I waited for the familiar cycle to begin. The profuse apologies. The excuses. The pleading promises that he didn't mean it, that it wouldn't happen again.

But this time, there was none of that.

"You're not going anywhere," he said quietly.

The words sent a cold shiver down my spine. There was no remorse in his voice, no panic. Just a cold, commanding presence that froze me in place.

This wasn't the same man I was used to. This was something different.

I moved carefully, my hands trembling as I continued gathering my things. I needed to get out. The atmosphere in the house shifted, growing heavier by the second.

"I'll call my dad," I blurted out, the words tumbling out before I could stop them. My voice cracked as I spoke, betraying the fear I was trying to suppress.

He laughed—a cold, mocking sound that sent another wave of panic through me.

"Call him," he said, smirking. "What's he going to do from Wales?"

His laughter echoed in the small space, cruel and cutting. He was right. My dad was hours away. No one could help me right now. I was alone, trapped in this house with a man who had no intention of letting me leave.

The fear hit me all at once—sharp, suffocating, all-consuming. I could barely breathe as my mind scrambled for a plan.

He was blocking the front door, his frame filling the doorway. I had one chance: the back door.

I moved quickly, forcing my feet to carry me toward the kitchen. My heart pounded in my chest, each beat a drum of urgency. I reached the door and fumbled with the lock, my fingers shaking uncontrollably. The old mechanism stuck, refusing to turn.

"Come on, come on," I whispered frantically, trying to force it open.

Before I could get the door unlocked, I felt the impact.

He slammed me against the door with such force that I gasped, the breath knocked out of me. Pain shot through my back and shoulders as I struggled to regain control. I could feel his breath against my neck, hot and furious.

"Shit!" I choked out, panic surging through me. My mind raced, desperate for a way out.

Adrenaline took over. I twisted, somehow breaking free from his grip, and ran for the front door with everything I had. My feet barely touched the floor as I moved, propelled by pure fear and instinct.

I reached the door and yanked it open, stumbling into the cool night air.

Behind me, I heard the sound of his fists slamming into the walls. Punch after punch. The plaster cracking under the force. His rage filled the hallway like a physical presence, suffocating and inescapable.

I dared a quick glance over my shoulder and saw him, his face contorted with fury as he pounded the walls.

Holes appeared in the plaster, evidence of his uncontrollable anger.

I didn't look back again.

I ran to my car, my breaths coming in ragged gasps. My hands trembled as I fumbled with the keys, locking the doors the moment I climbed inside. The sound of the locks clicking into place was the only thing grounding me in that moment.

And then I broke.

The tears came hard and fast, my body shaking with the force of the sobs. I gripped the steering wheel tightly, my knuckles turning white. I had held it together for too long. The fear, the shame, the exhaustion—it all poured out in that moment.

But I couldn't stay there.

I wiped my face with shaking hands, taking deep, uneven breaths. I couldn't let him win. Not now. Not after everything.

You won't see that hallway again. You won't see that door again. You won't see that driveway again.

I repeated the words in my mind like a mantra, forcing myself to focus. They gave me something to hold onto—something beyond the terror that still clung to me.

I started the car, the engine roaring to life.

I drove away without looking back. Tears blurred my vision, but I kept going. I didn't stop until I was far enough away that the house was nothing more than a distant memory in my rear-view mirror.

This time, I wasn't going back.

Chapter 13: A New Beginning

When I drove away that night, I wasn't just fleeing his house—I was shedding a skin, one that had clung to me like a suffocating second layer. Every mile that passed was a breath of fresh air filling lungs that had been starved for too long.

But even as the physical distance grew, the ghosts lingered. Fear stayed curled in the corners of my mind, like shadows waiting to pounce. I jumped at harmless sounds—footsteps behind me, a sudden knock, even the vibration of my phone. My body was conditioned to anticipate danger.

Yet something deep within me had shifted.

It was as though a part of me had already escaped before my feet ever crossed that doorway. The chains he had wrapped around my spirit had weakened, and I felt their weight lifting, link by link. For the first time in a long time, I could see the lie I had been living. The fog of manipulation, fear, and false hope was dissipating, leaving a painful clarity in its wake.

This wasn't survival anymore. It was a path forward.

I didn't launch into grand gestures of freedom. That wasn't how healing worked. I knew instinctively that I had to take small steps, one at a time. Quiet victories.

The first thing I did was start gathering evidence.

There was something empowering about it—laying out the truth in black and white, documenting every bruise, every message, every voice note filled with venom. Each piece was like a puzzle fragment, forming a picture I hadn't wanted to face before.

A photograph of the cuts on my leg, the bruise that bloomed like a dark cloud on my skin. Screenshots of messages designed to chip away at my sense of worth. Voice recordings of his voice—sharp and dangerous—echoing threats that once sent shivers down my spine.

At the time, I wasn't entirely sure why I was doing it. Maybe it was a subconscious survival mechanism, a need to arm myself with truth. Or maybe I knew that one day, I would need this evidence to prove—to others, but mostly to myself—that it had all been real.

The act of collecting these fragments became my quiet rebellion. He had tried to erase my reality, but I was reclaiming it, one painful reminder at a time.

That weekend, I found sanctuary in the warmth of friendship.

A friend had invited me over for a Sunday afternoon catch-up, and I hesitated at first. I had grown used to isolation, to hiding the full truth of my life behind smiles and deflections. But something inside me whispered that I needed this—needed to remember what it felt like to be seen without judgment.

We sat outside on her patio, sipping tea and chatting about everything and nothing. The late afternoon sun bathed us in its golden glow, a balm for my weary soul. We laughed about silly things—memories from our school days, the ups and downs of parenthood, the ridiculousness of everyday life.

For the first time in what felt like forever, I wasn't walking on eggshells. I wasn't hyper-vigilant, anticipating every shift in tone or mood. I could just be.

The simplicity of it was powerful. It reminded me of the life I had before him—a life that wasn't perfect but was filled with joy, connection, and light.

By the time I left that evening, I felt something stir within me. A sense of possibility.

That night, as I sat alone in my living room, I found myself scrolling through a dating app without much thought. It felt strange—like trying to speak a language I hadn't used in years. The profiles blurred together at first, faces and bios blending into a sea of unfamiliarity.

Self-doubt crept in, its voice insidious and persistent.

What are you doing?
Are you really ready for this?
Who would want you now?

The voice reminded me of all the insecurities I had carried since he first chipped away at my confidence. I pictured myself through his eyes—scarred, both physically and emotionally, a single mother with baggage that felt too heavy to unload.

But I silenced that voice, forcing myself to keep scrolling.

Then, unexpectedly, I matched with someone.

His profile was refreshingly normal—no red flags disguised as charm, no over-the-top bravado. Just simple, straightforward honesty.

I hesitated for a moment before sending the first message. The words felt awkward, like trying on shoes that didn't quite fit. But as the conversation unfolded, the awkwardness faded. We talked about everything—our jobs, our favourite places to travel, even our guilty pleasure TV shows.

It was light, unpressured, and exactly what I needed.

There were no expectations, no hidden barbs beneath his words. He didn't try to control the conversation or steer it in uncomfortable directions. It was just... easy.

And for the first time in years, I felt a spark of hope.

It wasn't a fairy-tale transformation. I wasn't suddenly free of fear or trauma. The wounds were still there, raw and tender beneath the surface. But this spark—this glimmer of possibility—was enough to keep me moving forward.

I thought back to all the breadcrumbs I had clung to in the past—the empty promises and fleeting moments of kindness that had kept me tethered to an illusion. This was different.

This wasn't survival. This was living.

I knew the journey ahead wouldn't be easy. There were still shadows to face, scars to heal. But I also knew one undeniable truth:

I was reclaiming my story.

And as I sat there, feeling the warmth of hope beginning to flicker in my chest, I thought of Pat's words once more. The candles meant to guide my path had been snuffed out when I wasn't ready, but now—finally—I could feel the first few beginning to glow, their flames steady and waiting to light the way forward.

Chapter 14: Shadows at the Door

I wanted to believe I was safe. I had done everything right— blocked him on every platform, removed him from every part of my life. I had distanced myself from the fear, the manipulation, and the memories. Slowly, I was learning to breathe freely again, rebuilding myself piece by piece.

For a while, it felt like I could leave the past behind. The warmth of new experiences, of laughter shared with someone who didn't try to control me, began to seep into my world. Hope glimmered faintly like the first few candles being relit, flames steady but fragile.

But trauma doesn't let go easily. It waits in the shadows, crouching low, waiting for moments of vulnerability.

That Saturday evening, the air was filled with anticipation and light-hearted excitement. My partner and I were getting ready to meet friends for drinks. The weekend buzz was in full swing, laughter from passing groups spilling into the night air as we walked toward the house.

"Let's pop in quickly," I said, smiling at him. "I just want to change my shoes."

We stepped inside, the house settling around us like a comforting embrace. I could hear my mum, brother, and sister-in-law chatting in the living room, their voices mingling with the familiar sounds of home.

The atmosphere was calm, relaxed—a stark contrast to the storm that was about to break.

"I won't be long," I said, heading upstairs. My shoes clicked softly on each step as I ascended, feeling peaceful in a way I hadn't in a long time. The happiness of the evening felt solid, like I could reach out and hold it in my hands.

But that peace shattered in an instant.

The chime of the Ring doorbell rang out, loud and intrusive, echoing through the house like a warning bell.

"I'll get it!" my sister-in-law called from downstairs.

I froze at the top of the stairs, a sudden chill washing over me. My pulse quickened. I didn't know why I felt so uneasy—just an instinctive tightening in my chest that whispered, something's wrong.

I stepped into my bedroom, pulling the curtain aside to glance through the window.

And that's when I saw him.

His eyes glared up at me from the driveway, cold and unrelenting. Time seemed to slow as dread clawed its way up my throat. My breath hitched, the familiar fear rushing back like a tidal wave.

"No," I whispered, shaking my head in disbelief.

This couldn't be happening. He wasn't supposed to be here. I had blocked him, cut him out of my life. But there he was, standing in the glow of the streetlight, his expression dark and menacing.

"Lock the door!" I screamed, panic surging through me as I backed away from the window.

Downstairs, my sister-in-law reacted instantly, locking the door and glancing outside through the peephole.

"He's not going anywhere," she muttered under her breath.

Her voice was steady, but I could see the tension in her posture. I had confided in her before—shown her the bruises, the messages, the voice notes—but I hadn't told my brother. Chris didn't know the full extent of what had happened. I couldn't bear to see the rage and helplessness in his eyes if he knew.

"Call the police," I said, my voice trembling.

She nodded and pulled out her phone. I heard her calmly relay the details to the dispatcher, her words clipped and precise. I half-expected him to leave when he saw her making the call. But of course, he didn't.

He stayed.

His posture was casual, almost mocking, as though the whole situation was beneath him. His shoulders shrugged lazily, and that smirk—that same fucking smirk—curved on his lips. It sent a fresh wave of nausea through me.

I had once believed in that smirk. Believed it meant charm, humour, something soft beneath the surface. Now, it was grotesque.

He hadn't changed. I saw him clearly now for what he was—a hollow, twisted man who thrived on control. And I hated myself for all the time I had wasted convincing myself otherwise.

"I'm going out there," I said suddenly, my voice low but firm.

My sister-in-law's eyes widened. "You don't have to. The police are on their way."

"I do," I replied. "This is my moment."

The cold night air wrapped around me as I stepped outside. I squared my shoulders, feeling a strange calm settle over me. He straightened when he saw me, his smirk deepening.

"You have no right to be here," I said, my voice steady and clear. "You don't control me anymore. You never will again."

His smirk faltered, confusion flashing across his face. I held my ground, refusing to let him intimidate me.

The words poured out—every truth I had held inside, every ounce of anger and hurt. I had spent too many nights choking on the things I wanted to say. Not tonight.

For the first time, he was the one caught off guard.

His shoulders stiffened, the defeat visible in his posture as he turned and began to walk away. I watched him go, my breath coming in ragged gasps. I had faced him and won.

As soon as I stepped back inside, my sister-in-law pulled me into a fierce hug. I collapsed into her arms, the weight of the moment crashing down on me all at once.

The tears came hard and fast, years of fear and tension finally releasing in a flood. I clung to her, sobbing uncontrollably. I had stood my ground, but the emotional toll was overwhelming.

"We've got you," she whispered. "You're safe."

We informed the others about what had happened, their shock quickly giving way to fierce protectiveness. My brother's expression darkened with barely contained fury. He clenched his fists, pacing the room as if searching for a way to act. My mum hugged me tightly, her eyes glistening with tears she tried to hold back.

The police arrived not long after, starting a new chapter of this ordeal—one that would require strength of a different kind.

But as I sat quietly in the aftermath, surrounded by those who loved me, I thought of Pat's words again.

"They lit candles to guide you, but your path was too broken. You weren't ready."

Now, those candles were finally flickering to life, their flames steady and determined. The shadows still loomed, but they no longer consumed me.

I was ready to walk forward.

This time, I wouldn't look back.

Chapter 15: Finding My Voice

I sat on the edge of the sofa, my hands still trembling slightly, as the police officer spoke calmly across from me. The room felt both too crowded and strangely empty at the same time. My mind buzzed with fragments of the night's events—his eyes glaring up at me from the driveway, the sound of his footsteps fading as he walked away, my sister-in-law's arms wrapped around me in a grounding embrace.

Now, here I was, trying to recount everything to the officer, my words stumbling out like shards of glass.

"And he… he wouldn't leave at first," I murmured, my voice thin and brittle.

The officer nodded, taking notes. His face was neutral, but there was something in his eyes—a quiet empathy that I hadn't expected.

My brother paced the room behind me, his frustration vibrating through the air. I could feel his protective rage simmering just below the surface, ready to erupt at any moment. I hadn't wanted him to find out this way. I hadn't wanted to burden him with the knowledge of what I'd endured. But there was no hiding it now.

"Why wasn't he arrested on the spot?" Chris demanded, his voice sharp. "He was trespassing, harassing her."

The officer remained calm, explaining the process with measured words. Something about needing more evidence and the need for restraint before escalating. Chris scoffed under his breath, shaking his head.

I didn't have the energy to argue. The night was stretching endlessly before me, every moment dragging like an anchor tied to my chest.

After the officer finished taking my statement, he typed something into his computer. A silence fell between us as he scanned the screen. Slowly, his posture stiffened, and he exchanged a glance with his colleague.

"What is it?" I asked, my voice suddenly tense.

The second officer leaned over to read the record on the screen. His face changed—eyes widening slightly, his mouth tightening into a grim line.

"Has he been in trouble with the police before?" I whispered, already knowing the answer but dreading confirmation.

"Yes," the officer said slowly, his tone more serious now. "Quite a history."

They didn't go into specifics, but I didn't need them to. I could see it in their expressions.

Then the first officer scrolled further. "There's a report here... an incident where he smashed car windows," he said, his voice neutral but pointed.

I froze, my heart sinking.

"Is that... is that you?" he asked, glancing up from the screen.

I nodded weakly.

His brow furrowed. "You didn't follow through with pressing charges."

"I know," I whispered.

"Why not?" he pressed gently.

It wasn't an accusation. I could tell he was trying to understand. But the question hit me like a punch to the gut.

Why hadn't I pressed charges? Why had I dropped it after everything he had done?

I wanted to explain how he had gotten inside my head, how the fear of retaliation and his psychological hold had kept me paralysed. I wanted to tell them how he had convinced me that I couldn't escape him, that no one would believe me, that I was better off keeping quiet.

But I couldn't find the words.

Instead, shame washed over me in waves.

I had been so vulnerable, so broken. How could I not have seen it? How could I have let him manipulate me like that?

Tears welled in my eyes before I could stop them. I tried to blink them away, but they kept falling. Quiet sobs shook my shoulders as the reality of it all came crashing down.

"I was scared," I finally managed to choke out.

The officer's expression softened. "It's okay. You're not the first person to feel that way."

His reassurance did little to ease the ache inside me. I wiped at my face, my hands shaking. I wasn't crying for him. I was crying for myself—for all the years I had spent trapped in fear and self-doubt. For the times I had convinced myself that I didn't deserve more.

But now... now I knew better.

The next day, I faced another round of questioning about the evidence.

I handed over the photos I had taken of the bruises and cuts—the ones I had snapped in secret, not knowing why I felt the need to document the damage back then. It had been instinctive, almost like an act of defiance in the midst of the fog. At the time, I didn't fully understand the weight those images would carry.

But now I did.

This was why I had kept them. Why I had saved the screenshots of his abusive messages and recorded the voice notes that haunted me.

Now was the time for them to be seen.

Each piece of evidence felt like a fragment of my past, exposed and vulnerable. But instead of drowning in shame, I allowed myself to feel something else—relief. These memories were no longer locked away inside me. They were out in the open, tangible proof of the hell I had survived.

Outside of the formalities, my support system rallied around me. Friends reached out, offering words of encouragement and love. Chris became an ever-present force of protection, checking in constantly and keeping a watchful eye on the house.

"You're not dealing with this alone," he said firmly one evening, his jaw clenched.

I knew it wasn't easy for him. He was trying to balance his anger and his need to protect me with the understanding that this was my fight. I appreciated that more than he knew.

And then there was my partner. He never pushed, never pried. He listened when I needed to vent and distracted me when I needed an escape. His quiet support was a balm to my frayed nerves.

One evening, as we sat together in the soft glow of the living room lamp, he gently took my hand.

"I've got you, babe... forever," he whispered, his voice warm and steady.

It was something he always said, but this time, it hit differently. Those words wrapped around me like a protective shield, melting the armour I had built around my heart. I had spent years being conditioned to expect conditions—to expect love that came with strings attached, with demands and threats.

But this was different. He didn't see me as broken or burdened. He saw me as someone who had survived.

As the days passed, the fear began to loosen its grip. It wasn't gone—trauma doesn't vanish overnight—but it no longer consumed me.

I found myself reflecting on that moment outside the house, when I had faced him down. The memory played on a loop in my mind—the steady tone of my voice, the way he faltered before walking away.

I had found my voice.

And then I thought of Pat's words.

"They lit candles to guide you, but your path was too broken. You weren't ready."

Now, those candles were no longer a distant promise. I could see them clearly—one by one, their flames flickering to life. They weren't fully lit yet, but they were beginning to illuminate the way. A path toward freedom, happiness, and healing stretched ahead of me.

The shadows still followed, but they no longer held the power to consume me.

This time, I wouldn't let them win.

Chapter 16: Candles on the Broken Path

Nothing about this chapter of my life feels final. It is unfinished, suspended in the limbo of police investigations and the looming possibility of court proceedings. The questions I once feared still hover in the distance, but I am not the same woman I was when this all began. I know now that I can face whatever is coming with a strength I never realised I had.

But that doesn't mean the road ahead isn't frustrating.

The police are slow, their processes tangled in bureaucracy and indifference. Information slips through the cracks, updates come in fragments, and I am left feeling powerless—just another case in an overcrowded system. Each unanswered call or vague response chips away at my patience, reminding me of the countless women who have walked this same broken path. Paths lined with jagged stones of doubt, mistrust, and fear, their footing unsure with every step.

Women who have tried to speak only to find that no one is truly listening.

The system sees these broken paths as barely significant. I hear it in the way they ask, Why didn't you leave sooner? Why didn't you press charges then? Questions that sting with implication, as though survival itself wasn't enough.

But I am done with shame. I survived because I did what I had to do.

Now, I'm here to mend that broken path—not just for myself but for others who follow. I'm here to relight the candles that were once extinguished in fear.

My strength doesn't come solely from within. It's fortified by the people who have stood beside me through this storm—my partner, my mum, my dad, my brother and sister-in-law, my children.

Chris, who has always been my protector, is still fierce in his anger but learns to hold back for me, knowing this is my battle to lead. My mum, even from miles away in Spain, listens with patience and love, her presence grounding me in a way I hadn't let her before. My sister-in-law remains a quiet force, always there when I need her.

And my partner—his words echo softly in my mind, anchoring me:

"I've got you, babe... forever."

This time, I believe it.

The boys, my reason for everything, fill my days with light and purpose. They don't know the full story, not yet, but they know their mum is stronger than ever. I see it in the way they smile at me, the way they reach for my hand without hesitation.

Their presence reminds me why I am here—to build a future for myself and for them that is free from fear.

The future feels like an open road, stretching far beyond the investigations and courtrooms.

For the first time in a long time, I know exactly where I'm headed.

I'm a teacher; it's what I've always done best. But this is different. The lessons I've learned through pain, fear, and survival aren't just for me. They're for the women who are still out there, still trapped, still silenced by shame.

I think of those broken paths again—the ones where women walk alone, surrounded by darkness, with no clear direction. I can see those paths now being illuminated. The candles are flickering to life, one by one, guiding the way forward.

My role now is to help others light their own paths, to help build a force of women who will not be reckoned with. Women who know their worth. Women who refuse to let anyone steal their power.

The breadcrumbs he once left me—the tiny moments of false hope and kindness that kept me trapped—are long gone now. Crumbled and swept away. What remains is the steady light of truth, resilience, and strength.

The shadows of my past still linger, but they no longer hold the power to consume me.

This path is mine now.

And this time, I'll keep walking it—with candles lit and my head held high.

Reflections

As I reach the end of this book, I find myself reflecting deeply on the journey that brought me here. There are no words that could fully capture the gratitude and love I have for the people who have stood by my side—my children, family, friends, and my partner. You have been my greatest support network, my light in the darkest of times. Your belief in me gave me the strength to rebuild when I thought all was lost. I thank you from the depths of my heart.

To my children: you are the reason I never gave up. You are my hope, my courage, and my greatest achievement. Every step forward I took was for you, to create a future where love and safety guide your path.

To my family and friends: thank you for your patience, your unwavering presence, and the times you reminded me who I was when I forgot. You have been my foundation when life felt unsteady beneath my feet.

To my partner: thank you for loving me without conditions, for showing me that tenderness and trust are not illusions but a reality I deserve. You remind me every day what healthy love truly is.

A special and heartfelt acknowledgment goes to Women's Aid. You were the supportive hand I needed when other doors were closed. Your guidance and understanding became a beacon in moments of overwhelming fear and confusion. When the police failed to provide the protection I so desperately needed, you were there to listen, to validate, and to empower. Your work changes lives and saves them.

This brings me to an important message for law enforcement. To those of you who handle cases of abuse: I urge you to do better. I understand that to you, this may be just one case among millions. But I promise you—it is not just a case to those living through it. Every woman, every survivor, is carrying the weight of her world on her shoulders when she comes forward to ask for your help. It is your duty to treat her with the urgency and respect she deserves. If you truly wish to see fewer cases of abuse...

Finally, to every woman reading this who has been made to feel small, isolated, or afraid: you are not alone. You never will be alone. There are people, strangers even, who care and who will stand with you. You are so much stronger than you think. Your worth is not diminished by the abuse you have endured. You have the power to reclaim your story, to find light beyond the shadows. And when you are ready, know that there are hands and shoulders waiting to help you through.

This book is for you.

With all my love and strength,

Useful Links and Support for Domestic Abuse Survivors

If you or someone you know is experiencing domestic abuse, there is help available. Below are some useful contacts in the UK:

- Women's Aid: www.womensaid.org.uk / 0808 2000 247 (24-hour helpline)
- Refuge: www.refuge.org.uk / 0808 2000 247 (National Domestic Abuse Helpline)
- National Centre for Domestic Violence (NCDV): www.ncdv.org.uk / 0800 970 2070
- Victim Support: www.victimsupport.org.uk / 0808 1689 111
- Men's Advice Line (for male victims): www.mensadviceline.org.uk / 0808 801 0327
- Galop (LGBT+ Domestic Abuse Support): www.galop.org.uk / 0800 999 5428
- Samaritans (for anyone in distress): www.samaritans.org / 116 123

You are not alone. Help is available, and support is just a call away.

Printed in Great Britain
by Amazon